Isn't My Name Magical?

SISTER AND BROTHER POEMS

Isn't My Name Magical?

SISTER AND BROTHER POEMS

BY James Berry

ILLUSTRATED BY Shelly Hehenberger

SIMON & SCHUSTER BOOKS FOR YOUNG READERS

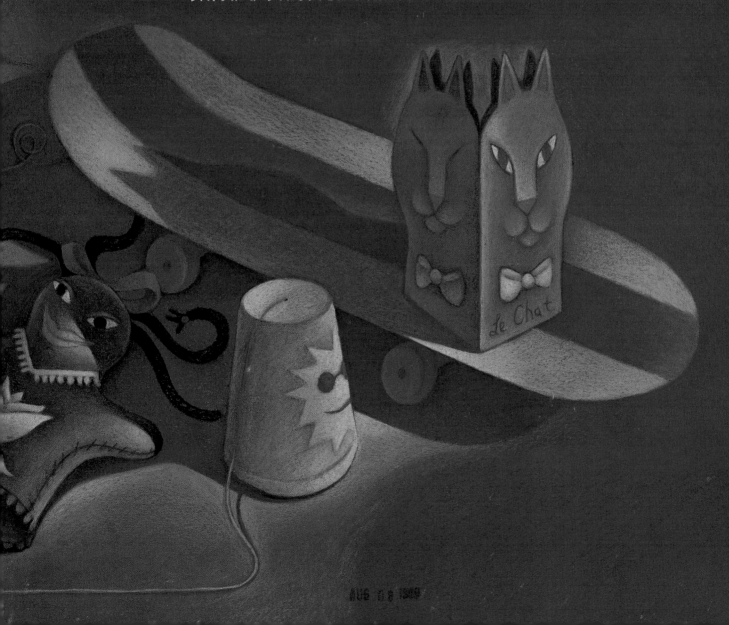

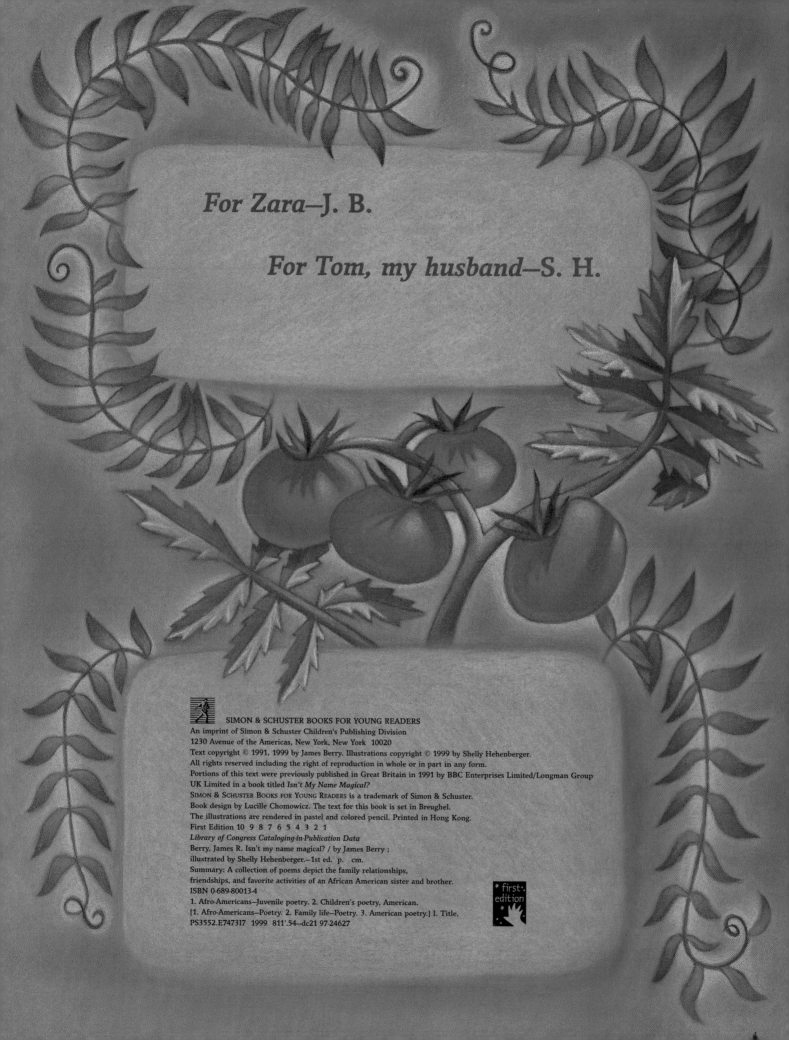

For Zara—J. B.

For Tom, my husband—S. H.

SIMON & SCHUSTER BOOKS FOR YOUNG READERS
An imprint of Simon & Schuster Children's Publishing Division
1230 Avenue of the Americas, New York, New York 10020
Text copyright © 1991, 1999 by James Berry. Illustrations copyright © 1999 by Shelly Hehenberger.
All rights reserved including the right of reproduction in whole or in part in any form.
Portions of this text were previously published in Great Britain in 1991 by BBC Enterprises Limited/Longman Group
UK Limited in a book titled *Isn't My Name Magical?*
SIMON & SCHUSTER BOOKS FOR YOUNG READERS is a trademark of Simon & Schuster.
Book design by Lucille Chomowicz. The text for this book is set in Breughel.
The illustrations are rendered in pastel and colored pencil. Printed in Hong Kong.
First Edition 10 9 8 7 6 5 4 3 2 1
Library of Congress Cataloging-in-Publication Data
Berry, James R. Isn't my name magical? / by James Berry ;
illustrated by Shelly Hehenberger.—1st ed. p. cm.
Summary: A collection of poems depict the family relationships,
friendships, and favorite activities of an African American sister and brother.
ISBN 0-689-80013-4
1. Afro-Americans—Juvenile poetry. 2. Children's poetry, American.
[1. Afro-Americans—Poetry. 2. Family life—Poetry. 3. American poetry.] I. Title.
PS3552.E747I7 1999 811'.54—dc21 97-24627

first
edition

Contents

8

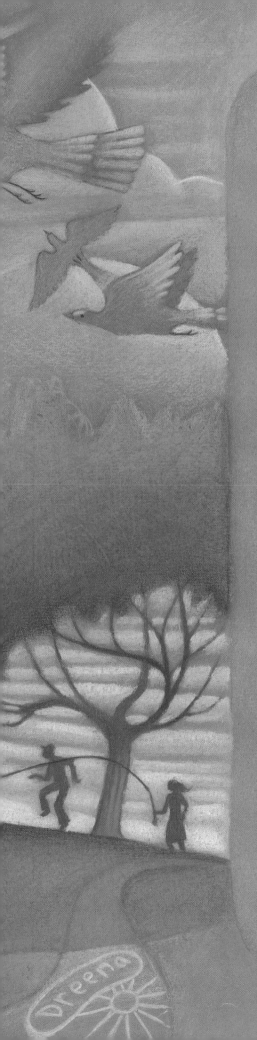

ISN'T MY NAME MAGICAL?

Nobody can see my name on me.
My name is inside
and all over me, unseen
like other people also keep it.
   Isn't my name magic?

My name is mine only.
It tells I am individual,
the one special person it shakes
when I'm wanted.

Even if someone else answers
for me, my message hangs in air,
haunting others, till it stops
with me, the right name.
   Isn't your name and my name magic?

If I'm with hundreds of people
and my name gets called,
my sound switches me on to answer
like it was my human electricity.
   Isn't that magical?

My name echoes across playground,
it comes, it demands my attention.
I have to find out who calls,
who wants me for what.
My name gets blurted out in class,
it is a terror, at a bad time,
because somebody is cross.

My name gets called in a whisper
I am happy, because
my name may have touched me
with a loving voice.
   Isn't your name and my name magic?

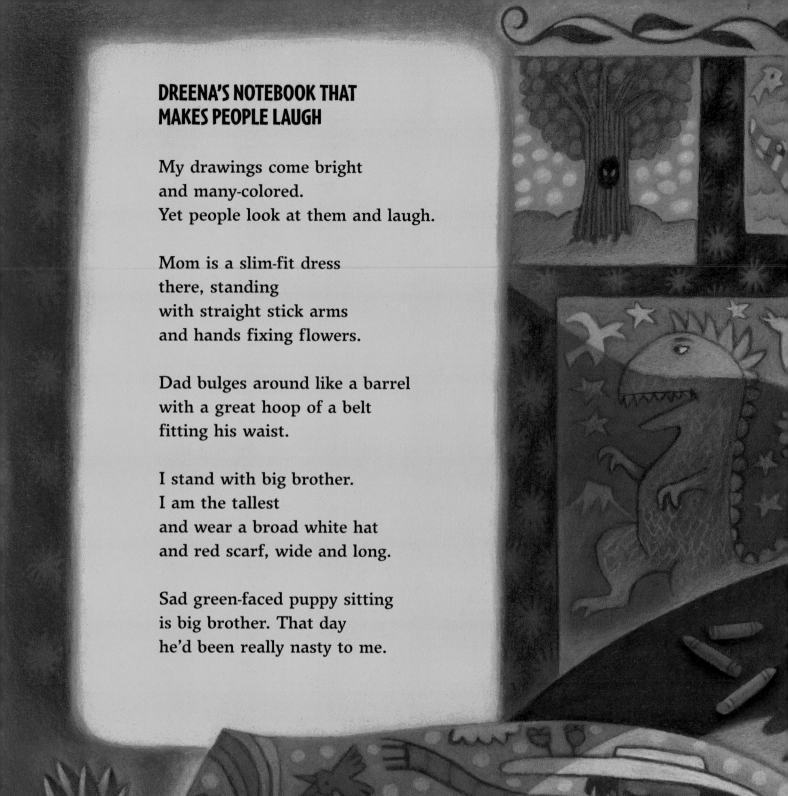

DREENA'S NOTEBOOK THAT MAKES PEOPLE LAUGH

My drawings come bright
and many-colored.
Yet people look at them and laugh.

Mom is a slim-fit dress
there, standing
with straight stick arms
and hands fixing flowers.

Dad bulges around like a barrel
with a great hoop of a belt
fitting his waist.

I stand with big brother.
I am the tallest
and wear a broad white hat
and red scarf, wide and long.

Sad green-faced puppy sitting
is big brother. That day
he'd been really nasty to me.

MY FAMILY OF PEOPLE

Dad

My daddy drives a train,
sometimes in a heavy jacket,
seeing wide landscapes
coming and coming and going.
Passing high hills that come
green, rocky, dusty, bare.
Rolling on to city sites
of dump wastes,
on to buildings towered up.
And, sometimes, Dad brings us gifts.
Sometimes, he plays our piano.

Mom

My mommy wears flat earrings
and flutters eyelashes
when she powders her face
and smells of a breezy perfume.
A teacher, Mom has lots of pens
and home and school jobs.
We play word games. And sometimes
each of us is a reader.
Then Mommy marks essay after essay.

Big Sister and Big Brother

Ziza plays her guitar
to her showpeople posters;
Delroy plays crazy faces to me
and his spacecraft pictures.

My sister sits
like fallen feather in a chair;
my brother drops
like body from upstairs.

My sister speaks quietly
for ears close;
my brother's voice is loud
all through the house.

My sister cooks
and the food gets left;
my brother's cooking goes down
like it's done by a top chef.

My sister rattles
right through her math;
my brother slumps over his
drawing that best-liked spacecraft.

My sister strums
and sings the blues;
my brother hurriedly pulls on
his running shoes.

Omi Rose

Her face was such a warm doll,
she had no strong legs to show
how her body was tall.

Then one day, tricky-eyed,
on her back there staring at me
she sized me up and smiled.

From then on—best buddies.
Coos and puffed-out cheeks.
Tickles. Splutters. Chuckles.

Mom breaks our too-much play.
Still, she looks on, as if to say,
"Come on quitter. Again!"
    Our baby—Omi!

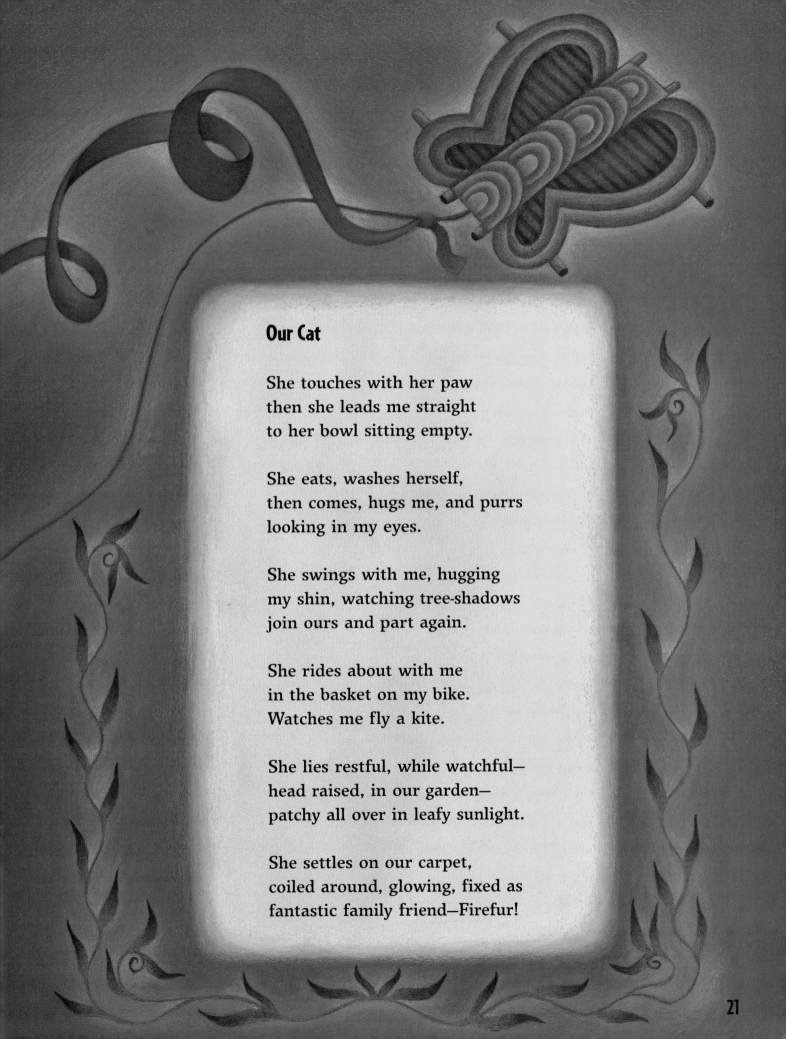

Our Cat

She touches with her paw
then she leads me straight
to her bowl sitting empty.

She eats, washes herself,
then comes, hugs me, and purrs
looking in my eyes.

She swings with me, hugging
my shin, watching tree-shadows
join ours and part again.

She rides about with me
in the basket on my bike.
Watches me fly a kite.

She lies restful, while watchful—
head raised, in our garden—
patchy all over in leafy sunlight.

She settles on our carpet,
coiled around, glowing, fixed as
fantastic family friend—Firefur!

DOESN'T A DIFFERENCE
MAKE FRIENDS TALK?

My dad watches a ball game
shouting vengeance;
Lyn's dad watches golf
in silent endurance.

We saw a man on the bus
with hair in his ear;
his lady beside him
kept a clean ear.

Oh the chased cat whizzed up
into a tree;
the dog managed only
two paws up the tree.

My dad goes all sandals
and feel-free in summer;
Lyn's dad's all a work show-off
with noisy lawn mower.

My class teacher is
shrieky and fussy;
our art teacher is cuddly
but isn't she messy?

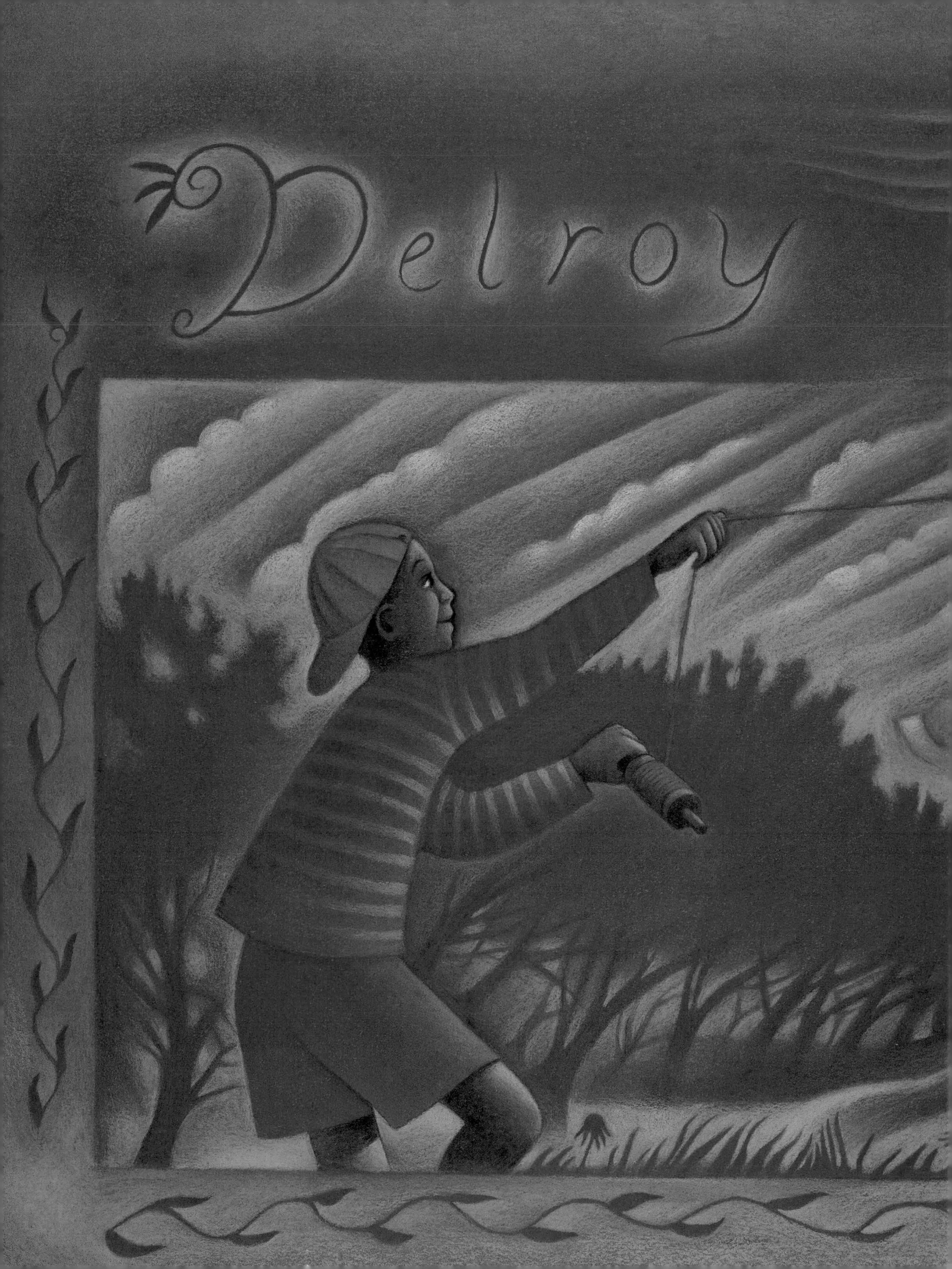
Delroy

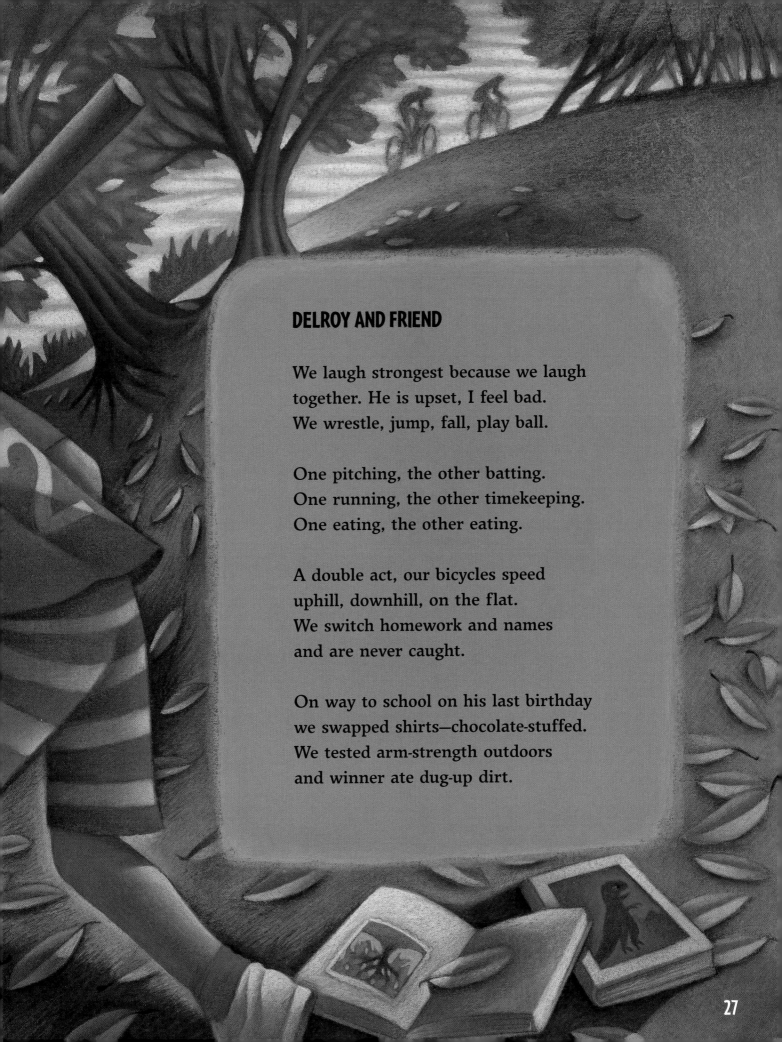

DELROY AND FRIEND

We laugh strongest because we laugh
together. He is upset, I feel bad.
We wrestle, jump, fall, play ball.

One pitching, the other batting.
One running, the other timekeeping.
One eating, the other eating.

A double act, our bicycles speed
uphill, downhill, on the flat.
We switch homework and names
and are never caught.

On way to school on his last birthday
we swapped shirts—chocolate-stuffed.
We tested arm-strength outdoors
and winner ate dug-up dirt.

DELROY THE DANCER-EXPLORER

I dance myself all clear
away from here—
for a boy skateboard flyer—
an underwater explorer.

In my deep sea gear
I have my deep sea flair.
I do my underwater walk
surrounded by sharks.

Again spinning on my top,
doing body-break and body-pop,
people start moving at once,
wheeling, hip-hopping, with dance.

And it's bodies full of joy—
with me the boy Delroy
a dancer-boy explorer.
    A dancer-boy explorer.

28

DELROY THE SKATEBOARD ROLLER

Sittn down is all immobility;
On my skateboard I show agility.
Out in the open a boy's ahright;
there's notn to him like takin flight.

Alone on my skateboard run
I'm havin some lonesome fun.
Here on my freetime ride
I leap and drop, I roll, I glide.

On playground flat my board makes circles;
In the air I hug Christmas parcels.
Joy of my board is its movement;
Without people it is contentment.

I want one owl on each my shoulder
hooting out as I leap each river.
Or I could have just one silent friend
To roll with, *calm calm*, without end.